Clint Faraday Mysteries 14
Dead End

Big trouble when some obnoxious arrogant bigots move onto Isla Popa. They want to build a marina. The Indios try to tell them it won't work there, because of natural conditions.

Pets and farm animals are being poisoned.

There is an attempt to murder a man.

What in *hell* is going on there?

Clint Faraday Mysteries
#14
Dead End

Contents

About the author

CD was born in Lakeland, Florida. His education is in genetics and botany. He has traveled over much of the world, particularly when he was in music as a rock rhythm guitarist with some well-known bands in the late sixties and early seventies. He has worked as a high steel worker and as a longshoreman, clerk, orchidist, bar owner, salvage yard manager and landscaper – among other things.

CD began writing fiction in 1984 and has more than 115 books published as of this time in SciFi, murder, orchid culture and various other fields.

He now resides in Bocas del Toro and David, Panamá, where he continues research into epiphytic plants. He loves the culture of the indigenous people and counts a majority of his closer friends among that group. Several have "adopted" him as their father. He funds those he can afford through the universities where they have all excelled. "The Indios are very intelligent people, they are simply too poor (in material things and money. Culturally, they are very wealthy) to pursue higher education."

CD loves Panamá and the people. He plans to spend the rest of his life in the paradise that is Panamá

- Estrelita Suarez V.

CD is involved in research of natural cancer cure at this time. It has proven effective in all cases, so far. It is based on a plant that has been in use for thousands of years, is safe, available, and cheap. He has studied botany, and was cured of a serious lymphoma with use of the plant, *Ambrosia peruviana*.

Information about this cure is free on the FaceBook page, Ambrosia peruviana for cancer. CD asks only that all who try it please report on its effectiveness on that group.

Dead End

Coin Dere

Clint Faraday, retired PI from Florida, was lounging in the hammock on his deck at his new permanent home on Saigon Bay, Isla Colon, Bocas del Toro, Panamá. He wasn't thinking of much, just allowing his mind to wander at will. Silvio Flores and family went by in their large cayuca (dugout boat). They greeted him with the common Indio greeting, "Coin dere!" (Good afternoon!). He waved and called the greeting back.

Judi Lum, his very attractive nextdoor neighbor from Taiwan, came onto her deck with Dave, their nutty musician/botanist/author friend. They greeted everyone. Judi called the Flores family over to her dock to give them pineapple upside-down cake she made for the kids, though everyone got a big piece.

Dave held up a plant to Clint. An orchid he'd brought back from the comarca. It was finally in bloom again. Dave called that it probably was a new species. It definitely wasn't listed as being found in Panamá.

Clint went to his piece of the plant (Dave had finally gotten him interested in the things and had his deck and yard covered with hundreds of species). It was a few days from blooming. An *Oncidium* alliance thing that Dave said was either a natural hybrid with a local *Oncidium* and *Psychopsis papilio* or a new species. Clint was even learning a few of the scientific names, though the Indios had local names for most of them. This one the natives in the comarca where it was found called it the Grande Mariposa Amarillo, or great big yellow butterfly.

He saw another one, a large spidery green and brown flower called *Brassia verucosa,* was blooming. He called to Dave that it was open. Dave said he'd come over. It was out of season, but that may be because he'd moved it. Maybe he'd cross it on his new species.

There was a loud call from Clint's front door, "Buenos!" that was the popular way to "knock" on a door here. He went out to find Ernesto and Pancho Smith standing there. He said, "Pase! Yantoro!" (all around greeting. It meant "good" – as did "Coin") and waved them in. Smith was a semi-common Indio name. Somebody's father or great grandfather was a gringo. They came in for Clint to offer them coffee or soda or whatever they liked. They accepted Cokes.

Dave came in with a plate of upside-down cake for everyone. Judi was with him, so they sat around the table on the deck to talk. Nesto and Pancho were beating around the bush, so Clint knew they needed a favor, but were uncertain about how to ask.

"What?" he asked. "You're friends. What's the problem? How can I help?"

"We are not certain," Nesto replied. "There is something very wrong on Isla Popa. We are not ... we cannot find what is happening. People are afraid, I think because those people want to buy the back end where there is deep water to build a marina and they think we don't want a marina there. We are only trying to say it would not be a good place for a marina. No one would come. There is no connection to anywhere else and there is no tourism on Popa because of that. It would mean jobs for us, but that is no good if it will fail."

"Why are you afraid? Of what or whom?"

"We are not afraid. Others are, those who live very close

to where they want to construct the marina," Pancho answered. "Their cows have died for no reason. The chickens are not laying, and are very nervous, even for birds. The parrots don't come there where they used to come, many hundreds of them, to roost in the big trees.

"We do not say those people are doing it. It is that there was no such thing before they came. There was no problem until they started making the marina, now there are many problems. We do not have much money. We wanted to ask that you find what is wrong and who is doing things, as a friend. We have waited too long, already."

"Violeta's from there. She told me they had two cows that died and a pig. They didn't know why," Judi said. "They live on the west end of the island. Is that where they want to build the marina?"

"Yes. Violeta is the daughter of Samos and Irena. They are close to the place," Nesto replied.

"You should have come to Clint before. She told me that a month or more ago."

"I'll see what's happening out there. If there's some bunch of greedbags doing anything to your stock, I'll put a fast end to it," Clint promised. "Those tactics are from the past. Try them now, and we'll teach them a lesson in respect!" Clint always got furious when asshole gringos – or anyone else, for that matter – tried to intimidate the Panamanians, particularly the Indios. He was such a close friend to them that Obilio, a chief on the comarca, had declared he was Ngobe (the Indigenos in Bocas del Toro Province). He was, therefore, by law, an Indio. Ngobe. (NhOBEh. The language is much like Guayme (WHY-me).

Clint got all the information he could from them and

promised to go down to Popa the following morning to talk with other natives, then he'd go calling on the gringos.

Clint pulled up to the dock near the Smith's cluster of houses. Six small kids ran down to hug him and call him Tio Clint. He went toward the houses. Four more from the neighboring houses came running to hug him. They were the Taylor family, also a common Indio name.

Pancho came out to greet him with his wife, Marta. They talked a bit over fresh ground coffee from the finca. Clint was filled in as much as they knew, but he would walk across to the Serrano place to talk with people who were actually involved, then he'd go to where he could see a dock being built. That would be the marina. He knew a thing or two about the area that whoever was building that place didn't, apparently. It was no place for a marina, even if there were access to the mainland or major islands.

"They don't speak much Spanish and don't care to learn. That kind," Samuel said, a little later, when Clint strolled over to his place with a gaggle of kids skipping along with him. "We try to tell them they can't build a successful marina there because it is the wrong place. They are very nasty and bravo and say we can't tell them where to build or not build anything because they have a permit.

"What good is a permit if the place is wrong?

"They are not very nice people. The son is maybe worse than them. He doesn't want to be here. He wants to go back to Oklahoma, where he was raised. The boys here tried to be his friend, but he is not interested. He doesn't want any friends, then I have heard him saying to his parents that there is nothing to do here and no one will even talk to him. I think the woman also does not want to be in Panamá. She says no one will be her friend.

"How can we? They won't talk to *us!*"

"I know the type," Clint said. "All us gringos have to live with what they make people think all gringos are."

"We don't think of people in that way. Some gringos are like them and some are not – the same as there are Indio thieves, but most are not. Besides which, you are no longer a gringo. You are Ngobe!"

"And proud to be!" Clint returned. "I'll see what I can do. Maybe I can make them realize you aren't telling them they can't build there because of what you want, but because the natural conditions make it stupid to try."

They chatted a bit more, then Clint and the kids went back to his boat. He hugged them all goodbye and motored around to the dock under construction. It had signs that said it was a private dock. Keep out. Clint ignored the signs and tied his boat next to a large material hauler barge. He went onto the dock and up to the house, where a man, woman and teenage boy were standing, watching him. He greeted them and introduced himself.

"I'm Robert, this is Sarah and my son is William. Morris. From Oklahoma, in the states. I've heard of you. You're Clint Faraday, the bigshot retired detective."

"I'm a retired detective. I'm no bigshot. I just keep my hand in the business because the police here asked me to.

"You're building a marina, I understand. I think there are some things you don't know about the area you've chosen."

"Here we go! More threats about what will happen if we try to open anything here among the Panamanian apes!" William said, sourly. "Go fuck yourself!"

"You're a real wise-ass little snotty bastard, aren't you?" Clint said, pleasantly. "I get so damned tired of your type of punk. You think you know everything and that the world revolves around your ass. You'll learn.

"I think you totally misunderstand what the Indios are trying to tell you, but that's mostly because you don't have the self-respect to understand them. You react to them the way you react to anyone you don't understand."

"But you do understand them!" William spat. "You're no Indian!"

"Actually I am. I'm a Ngobe. I understand a lot more than you might think.

"Why do you people stand there and allow this spoiled little punk to talk to your guests like this? Is it the way you were raised, so you don't know that discipline has a lot to do with how your life turns out?"

"He's just going through that stage," Sarah answered. "It doesn't do any good to talk to him. He's just rebellious and doesn't like it here. He'll outgrow it."

"If he survives. Are you willing to listen to a few facts, or do you prefer to act the victim of something undefined you don't want defined? It's *you* who stand to lose your asses here. The Indios have been here since before the Americas were discovered. They'll be here when we finally are able to destroy what we call civilization with our greed."

"You know, I don't like your attitude at all!" Robert said, haughtily. "You aren't going to scare us off this place! Don't bother trying!"

"Okay. I'll go away and let the natural facts of this area break you. I don't much care for your attitude, either, in case you're stupid enough to think I'm impressed with it. If you'll stop to think for ten seconds, you'll see that I have nothing to gain or lose by coming here. I'm impressed by your actions and words, but not the way you probably intended.

"'Bye!

"Oh! One other thing. If anymore animals are poisoned or such, you'll find that I'm a police officer, when called. I'll have the two of you locked up for ninety days. You can refuse to allow a minor like this little half-assed punk to be prosecuted. He can see how he likes living for ninety days in a place he's alienated everyone, without you to pamper him."

"We haven't poisoned any animals! What are you talking about?!" Sarah cried.

"So. You have a run-in with the locals because you don't understand what they're trying to tell you and their animals start dying off by mere coincidence. Get real!"

"I assure you, we wouldn't do anything like that! Why would we poison animals because we can't get along with people?"

William was looking at his feet and shifting back and forth.

"Your little punk would, and did, though. You're held responsible, if you won't allow his prosecution."

Robert turned on William. "Did you poison anyone's animals? – And don't lie to me! I'll teach you a lesson that you'll never forget!"

"They hate me! They made me do it!" William screeched. Robert slapped him hard enough that he went down.

"Okay, Faraday. I swear before god we didn't know anything about that! *Why* would you do something like that, William? We are *not* that kind of trash!"

"I wanted to make them make us leave! I *hate* it here! I don't have any friends and there's nothing to do!"

"You can't have friends if you refuse to be a friend," Clint said. "You don't have any idea of what your stupid selfish acts have done. The Indios won't make you leave, you'll put your parents in a position where they have to leave because they've lost their asses in a stupid venture that wasn't researched nearly enough," Clint lectured.

"Listen, Faraday. I swear to you we didn't know anything about this! No wonder they want us out! I would, too!

"Okay. Maybe we've been stupid not to listen, but I swear, we thought they were threatening us!

"What do you mean about the research? We bought this place because there was a permit for a marina here. Collins, from the company in Panamá City, said it was all researched and that there's plenty of business for two or three more marinas here! The water's deep enough around here for some large draft boats and it's level enough for two hundred feet to build a good dry dock. The marinas at Almirante and on Bocas are full all the time, to where they anchor all around the bay, close.

"Besides the fact that we're resented by the natives, what's wrong with building a marina here?

"I know what the Indios say about not having entrance to the mainland or Bocas, but they use their dingys to come and go *now*! What are we missing? Exactly? What makes it a bad idea?"

"The large draft bit."

"There's plenty of water in here!"

"And plenty out there. It's between that doesn't have a channel. There's plenty here and plenty there, it's just not connected. There's nowhere close where you can come in here, drawing more than three or four feet of water. The Indios weren't saying they would keep boats from coming here, they were saying the boats *couldn't* come because of the natural features of the place."

"But the man from Panamá City assured us that there was plenty of water and that boats come and go here all the time!"

"Fishing boats. Tour boats, less than twenty six feet. Catamarans and tri-hulls that don't draw more than two or three feet of draft. Those aren't live ons, except the catamarans. No one keeps fishing boats in a marina that they can't get to without a boat half the size they have. The catamarans anchor among the islands and move a little every day to get by the anchorage laws."

"Oh, dear God!" Sarah whined. "We thought we'd covered everything! This is terrible! Our investors will be livid!"

"Get off the attitude and learn to listen to people living in the area. They're the ones who know the conditions, not some schnook who's trying to sell you something so he gets a big commission."

"Well, I think I've learned something, but it's not about the Indians, it's about land sales here in Panamá," Robert said, dejectedly. "He's the one who said the Indians will try to get us out. They hate gringos."

"No, they don't. They would even like to see a successful operation of some type here. It would mean jobs."

Sarah looked shocked. "But ... but ... My God! That's true! They don't have any jobs on these islands! We'd bring them some! My God!"

"They have plenty of jobs, here. They're mostly working for themselves, growing coffee and cacao or cows and pigs this little snit poisoned. They're not about money, they're about living the lifestyle the people are used to and like."

"They aren't interested in money? Get real! They gouge us every chance they get! We even got taken for six bucks by the taxi when we first came here. Nothing's changed! Every time we go to Bocas, we get screwed!"

"Two little things. That's not the Indios, here, it's Panamanians, mostly the blacks, because they feel the gringos owe them something. Number two, your attitude will make anyone, anywhere, want to stick it to you as much as they can.

"I'll go. Just remember that the people here were trying to warn you that it wouldn't be smart to sink a lot of money into a project that was doomed before it got started."

"I've learned my lesson," Robert said. "I'm through listening to ... even some of my own family. I wasn't an only child and didn't get the coddling this, as you would say, little spoiled brat's used to.

"You'd better get used to things going a lot harder on you, sonny boy. Poisoning these people's animals crossed the line – a long way. You're going to pay these people for every cow and pig you did that to."

"I can't pay them! I don't have anything to pay them with! Besides, they asked for it!" he snarled.

This time he ducked just fast enough to miss another hard slap.

"Your allowance is twenty bucks a week. I figure no allowance for two years will handle it!" Robert snarled.

"Ma!" William squealed.

"Now, Robert. He was just rebelling. Don't be too hard on him," Sarah wheedled.

"I'm not being hard enough! You won't get me to let him get away with this shit, anymore! My God! We're about to lose everything we have and you want to protect the one who caused most of it! If we'd listened, from the first, we wouldn't have borrowed – how will we ever pay that back?"

"We'll just have to sell this place and move back to Oklahoma," Sarah said, almost happily. William smirked.

"I see," Clint said. Robert looked a little shocked. He stared hard at Sarah. Clint wouldn't be at all surprised if he slapped her as hard as he'd slapped William.

"There's a little problem with that," Clint said, to ameliorate the tension. "This place was for sale for ten years or more when it was unloaded on you. There were other buyers, but they researched it among the people here, not a bunch of sleazy crooks in Panamá City. They decided to run, not walk, away from the deal. I doubt you'll find anyone to buy it for another ten years."

That got rid of the smirks!

"Oh, fucking shit!" Robert exclaimed.

Clint got in his boat, waved and headed back to Bocas Town.

"Buenas!" Pancho called from Clint's front door, three mornings later. Clint called, "Yantoro! Pase!" and Pancho came in.

"What's cooking?" Clint asked.

"Cooking? I am not cooking anything. This is your house and ... oh! An expression!

"I think there is going to be big trouble on Popa. Those people again. Someone tried to kill the husband. The wife and that unspeakable son are blaming the Serranos."

"What happened?"

"Well, the husband was working by the dock, trying to take out some kind of winch he was returning to the place where he bought it. His back was turned and someone hit him with a piece of steel rod like they use in concrete. He was hit more than one time, but it wasn't hard enough to kill him. Anton heard the noise when he yelled and went over, but whoever did it was gone when they heard him coming. He called Enrique and me and we went to help. We tried to make the husband come to the hospital. He acts like he doesn't hear or know what's happening, at times and is dizzy.

"Clint, we get along with him very well, now. He has paid for the dead animals and says he was a fool to believe when they told him we would try to make them leave. We are better to him than his own family is. It is not he who accuses, it is the wife and son.

"I think, if any of my sons are like that one, I will kill him, myself!"

"Who did it? Do you know?"

"No. No one was there. Just him and his wife and son."

"I'll go get him and make him go for X-rays. He's acting like he has a serious concussion or a fracture. Would you like to come along?"

He nodded. Clint locked the front and went through to his boat. He and Pancho headed for Popa.

"You! What are you doing here? You are not welcome on my property!" Sarah yelled.

"It's not your property. It's registered under a corporate name. You're merely the recording secretary in the corporation," Clint replied. "Where is Robert?"

"He's sleeping! One of these Indians tried to kill him!" William said. "No Indian is to come on this property. I'll have them arrested! Get out!"

"Go fuck yourself, punk!" Clint snapped back. "You're a minor and can't give any orders about anything, here. I'm a cop who's come because there's a report of a serious injury as the result of a murder attempt. It's the Indios who're trying to help him, not his family. That will bear some investigation.

"Where is he? Now! I'll run your ass in for obstruction in a heartbeat, punk!"

"Ma!"

"Her, too," Pancho said. "She's responsible for the way you act here."

"Maybe that would be best," Clint said, but it wouldn't do any good. Neither of those two spoke Spanish, though they both seemed to know what he'd said. Clint pushed past the two and went to the house to call, "Robert? Clint Faraday here! Can I come in?"

"Yes, please," came back. "I think I'm worse than I think I'm worse than I ... I can't think."

"I'm taking you to the hospital in Bocas for X-rays,"

Clint said. "Do you need help walking?"

"I can't ... I'll trust you. I have a little trouble walking."

Pancho helped him stand, then had him put an arm under his shoulder to help him get to the boat. He was extremely shaky and pale. Clint started the boat with Sarah and William screeching at him that he had no right!

Clint got his cellular and called to Sergio, the police captain. He said to get the ambulance to the ferry dock and to alert Doc that there was a case of a probable skull fracture and as probable, poisoning. He pushed the boat as fast as he could. He got to the dock in about fifteen minutes. Doc was there and took a quick look before they put him in the ambulance. He said it was a depressed skull fracture and there might be other things. Part of this wasn't at all symptomatic of a skull fracture.

After Robert was hauled away, Clint went back to his place and tied to the dock. Judi came over and asked what was going on. Pancho said he thought the wife or son or both tried to kill the husband. Clint filled in the spaces for her.

"Judi, have you heard anything about those people? Anything since I went out there four days ago?"

"Well, Violeta was at the community action meeting. We talked about it. There are people from all the islands where there's any kind of community. Even from Isla Pastore and Renacimiento. They all said they thought those people were fools and that there was going to be more trouble because of what someone else had said or something.

"I think that Grossman character, who came in yesterday afternoon, is somehow involved. He booked rooms for two other couples in Swan's Cay. They're supposed to be here today. He was asking Lucy and Angela about the Morris people."

"Judi, you can get so much more information so much faster than the cops or myself, I can't believe it! Thanks!"

They chatted and visited for another hour, then Clint said he was going to the hospital to talk with Doc. Pancho had to get back home. Judi had the garden club meeting.

"What's the projection, Doc?" Clint asked, when he was in the office at the hospital.

"Depressed skull fracture that could have gotten worse to the point of fatality," he answered. "I think there's some kind of poisoning, maybe ethylene glycol. It's badly dehydrating him. I can counter it. He'll live, but there may be brain damage from the fracture. I can hope not, but ... we'll see. I've relieved the pressure and he's in very good physical condition. He keeps saying 'It can't be. I don't believe it. It can't be,' over and over, at times. He also says, 'Fatty? That was Fatty. When did he come?' and things like that. He's confused about what happened, and sometimes can't remember where he is, or why."

Clint took out his cellular and called Judi, who was at the meeting. "Is Grossman fat?" he demanded.

"Grossman? Who ... oh. Yes, but not extreme. You tend to think he's fatter than he is when you hear the name. Grossman. He's a little fat. Maybe twenty pounds overweight at five eight, so it shows around the gut.

"Just a sec." She talked with someone for a minute, then, "Yveth says Grossman went out with Maxie, yesterday afternoon late. They didn't get back until after dark. You know how Maxie is about being on the water after dark, with so many boats that don't have running lights.

"Help any?"

"As usual, a lot," Clint replied. "Thanks, Jude. You're amazing!"

"Yeah, I know. By accident."

They said their goodbyes. Clint told Doc he wanted to talk with Maxie about something. "Put Morris somewhere he can be protected. I won't be surprised if there's another attempt on him, here."

Doc nodded and said he'd be put where no one could get to him, even if they knew where it was.

"Make careful note of anyone who asks about him. Anyone at all."

"Doesn't need saying. Complete with pictures from the new videocams in the halls and such."

Clint went down to the docks, then back to the trail the natives used, next to the Barco Hundido. Maxie was loading some staples for Bastimentos. Grossman had gone to Pastore, then Popa. He got off the boat on Popa and was gone for about half an hour. That was why it was dark when they got back.

Crap! Now there's another suspect! Clint would have been much happier to only have Sarah and William.

He went to the police station to discuss matters with Sergio, then back to the hospital, where everything was quiet. Then he went home to handle his e-mail and start a Google Search for Sarah and William Morris from Middletown, Oklahoma.

He then did a search on Grossman, but didn't have enough information to get a start. He then repeated on Yahoo! and other engines.

How stupid! He called the Swan's Cay to ask about Grossman. Solomon Samuel Grossman. He then got the names of the two expected couples. Ellen and Francis Greenwood and Fanny and Edward Auermond.

He did the searches on all of them. They were normal enough types, it seemed. Sarah had been in trouble as a teen, when she tried to run another girl over with her father's car. The girl had taken her boyfriend. It went to PTI and was silenced. William had been in some trouble three times for petty theft and underage drinking, plus a minor pot possession thing that didn't go anywhere, after Sarah intervened and assured the court that it wouldn't happen again because it was the fault of his peers. He wasn't going to be around that bunch, anymore. It seemed Mama was always stepping in to keep junior out of trouble. She wasn't going to be of any help to him, here. She could stop prosecution of a minor, but that would mean she accepts all the financial and legal responsibility. That was no joke in Panamá, with these kinds of cases.

Clint sat back and wondered how he was going to find who was the action figure and who was the schemer. This was one sick sordid bunch of people. Milton Goldstein came over for a beer or two and said Clint might be in for some headaches. There were a bunch of people coming. People who as much as worshiped money. They were Jewish and the kind of people the decent Jews despised for what they made everyone in the world think of Jews.

"I know the type," Clint said. "I'm stuck in dealing with some of them, now."

"Robert's not so bad. It's that damned scheming bitch and that whiny half-assed spoiled brat of theirs. Robert, you can get through to, but not when he's around those two. I think he's finally opening his eyes about them. He was telling me, night before last, that he thinks they're the cause of all his troubles with the natives. He's finally listening to them. He sees they weren't putting him down or threatening him, they were trying to stop him from making a huge mistake.

"He knows the mistake's already made, that it's his own

fault for listening to family and so-called friends. He's actually getting along with two or three of the Indios out there."

That was much the same as Clint was beginning to believe.

"Quiet night. No one came to do anything except someone named Grossman. All he wanted to know was if Morris was alright. I told him it was too soon to tell. He'll wait to do anything, that way, if he's part of this," Doc explained. Clint nodded.

"He's part of it, but I have no idea what part. Yet.

"Is he anymore coherent this morning?"

"A bit. He's still confused and weak. It was ethylene glycol. Antifreeze. Tastes like sugar, so they were able to put a little in his coffee or something. It would have eventually killed him, if they kept it up. Somebody knows how to use it to make it look like something else, when you're not looking for a specific."

"I think they wanted to make him have to go back to the states, where he'd die, so they can collect insurance, or something. I believe there was a term policy in the corporation papers. I'll look that up.

"Grossman and four people who are coming today are officers in the corporation."

They chatted a few minutes, then Clint went home and to his computer to trace insurance policies. All of them had policies stating the major players' debts would be paid off and the corporation would collect two million if they died of natural causes.

So. That was probably why the injuries weren't immediately fatal. What they apparently didn't know was that he would have died of those injuries if they'd continued the poison. No insurance company would pay if it was directly connected to a murder attempt. It would be too easy to show that was the immediate cause, the sickness and debilitation would be considered part of the attempt. They would very definitely look for poison, if there had been an attempt on the subjects life!

Clint heard the flight from Panamá City coming in, so got on his motorcycle and raced to be there when the passengers deplaned. He considered the man waiting by the door was probably Grossman, there to meet them.

Two more people got off near the first and waved at Grossman. Two more got off a few people later and did the same. He went to the baggage checkout and stood, talking animatedly with the four, then got a taxi to take the bunch to the Swan's Cay. They checked in and went to the restaurant to ask the waiter something, then took a table to the side.

Clint wasn't dressed to be inconspicuous in that restaurant, so waited near the door. He could see them at an angle through a window, so moved to the side and waited about twenty minutes, until Sarah came in. She went directly to them and said something. They got up and headed for the door.

Clint would be recognized by her, very definitely, so stayed back and out of sight. They got two taxis and headed toward Saigon Bay, so Clint followed at a distance on the bike. They stopped at the hospital.

Clint took out his cellular and called Doc, who was at the morgue on one end of the hospital grounds. He said he'd be over there in less than two minutes. He'd call the receptionist and tell her to stall them by saying she had to check with his doctor before she could allow visitors.

Clint saw Doc go from the morgue to the side door of the hospital and in. He waited two minutes, then went in, himself. Trina pointed to the door to Doc's office and raised an eyebrow. Clint rolled his eyes and barged into the office.

"You don't knock when ... oh, hello, Faraday. What can I do for you?"

"I wanted to say something to Mrs. Morris. Bob saw her come in here and called me. I was just down the street, so here I am."

"I don't have anything to say to you! You kidnapped my husband from my house! I want charges to be filed against you for that! So there!"

"Mr. Faraday and Mr. Smith brought Mr. Morris here yesterday in a condition requiring immediate action, or it would have proven fatal," Doc declared, sternly. "He explained what had transpired. He was acting as agent for the Policia Nacional and, with what I have learned through treatment of Mr. Morris, can arrest you here and now for criminal neglect – at best! (Clint shook his head the least bit.) I am conducting tests on unexplained symptoms on a man who someone tried to murder. You will not see him until those tests are completed. If you try further to obstruct medical treatment of a man who was almost killed for one more instant, I will demand that Mr. Faraday, as an agent for the Policia Nacional, arrest the bunch of you. Immediately!

"Is that quite clear?"

"Now, let's not push this thing out of hand," Grossman said. "We're concerned because we're partners in a company building some facilities on Isla Popa. We've invested a great deal in the venture and want to know what he did or didn't accomplish, so that we may recoup our funds, if what we've learned is true."

"So? It's about money? You're not concerned that your partner was almost murdered?" Doc asked.

"Of course we're concerned!" one woman cried. "Do

you have any idea of how much *money* is at stake here? Do you have the least conception of how much we've invested in something that might destroy that money?"

"It's the money, not the patient?" Doc asked.

"He's a partner in a business. We're naturally concerned with the business. We hardly know Morris, personally. We're not wealthy. We've invested our entire savings in what seemed a very solid project. Now we may lose it all! *Of course* it's about the money!" One of the men said.

"You are?" Doc asked.

"I'm Mr. Greenwood. This is my wife, Mrs. Greenwood. We are investors."

"We're Mr. & Mrs. Auermond."

"I'm Mrs. Morris!" Sarah snapped, "As if Clint Fuckoff doesn't know that!"

"That's *Mr*. Fuckoff, to you," Clint fired back.

"I'm Sol Grossman. We're just upset by this. Please excuse our apparent rudeness (a sharp look at Sarah), but we stand to lose more than we can really afford. You people don't understand the importance of security or the handling of large sums."

"I think Mr. Faraday understands a tiny bit about handling funds," Doc said. "He donated several million dollars to help this and some other hospitals, as well as some millions for schools and clinics."

"UH! *Millions*?!" Greenwood cried. He looked like he'd just received a hard punch in the gut. "That is, we've invested a bit more than a million dollars in this project. We certainly don't have millions to throw around in, er, for charity or whatever."

What Doc didn't tell them that the millions Clint was credited with giving was parts of deals when he caught criminals. Though he could have claimed it, he didn't care for more than enough to get by. He considered people who wanted money for the sake of money to be shallow to empty.

"Hell! You spent over six million on that new hospital near Puerto Armuelles alone, didn't you?" Doc asked, trying to hide the laughter in his voice. The Auermonds and Grossman were sitting there with their mouths hanging open. Sarah was about to faint. Grossman was trying to control his expression.

"Something like that. It was a fairly large project. It's not important, here," Clint replied.

"The Indians said you built the clinic on San Cristobal with some Mathews person, but we thought it was only a little hut with a doctor every week or something," Sarah wheedled. "We had no idea! We would have listened to you from the first if we'd known you have practical business experience!"

"I don't have business experience," Clint said. "Let's get back to Robert. You can't see him until Doc okays it. Don't make pests of yourselves. He couldn't care less about your investments. He's concerned with the patient."

"Well, I suppose, if he's getting proper care, we'll just have to wait," Grossman said.

"Mr. Faraday, I want you to know we didn't know you were a person of quality or we would never have acted the way we did," Sarah said. "I'm afraid we haven't met many who we could relate to here and, just perhaps, we became too hard in our outlook. We were suspicious, you see. Everyone seemed to be trying to get money from us. They will steal anything not welded to the floor!"

So now Clint was a person of quality. He had money.

He took a deep breath and suggested they all calm down and stop over-reacting. They could wait until Doc said they could talk with Robert. There wasn't really anything else to do.

A lot of, "Oh, well! Guess you're right about that, old sock! Hearty good fortune and all that rot, eh what? Got to relax and go with the flow!" Clint could have puked. All of a sudden he was the greatest guy in the world and a true friend who was only trying to help!

They soon filed out. Clint got on the bike and rode around back until they got in taxis and left, then went back to Doc's office.

"Do you believe those people? Can anyone be that totally devoid of character?" Doc asked. "I get them like that. Not usually so extreme."

"Want to try to talk with Morris?"

"Can he?"

"He's a lot better. I think he'll be alright."

They went to his room. He was looking a lot better.

"It was Clinton? Frank Clinton?" Robert asked, when they came into the room.

"Close. Clint Faraday."

"I'm still pretty confused about a lot of things."

"Let it come back naturally. Don't try to force it," Doc suggested. "I have to get back to work. If you get tired, tell Clint to take a hike."

Robert grinned, and waved. Clint pulled a chair close to the bed and asked what he remembered.

"I was doing something by the dock and suddenly there were lights exploding and a lot of pain, then nothing except little flashes until I woke up here this morning. I seem to remember a boat and ... Pancho! Pancho was helping me. Someone was trying to hit me again ... who I couldn't see. There was someone in another boat. A blue one. One of those tour boat things.

"That's about it."

"Fatty?" Clint asked.

"Fatty? I don't think ... he was in the other boat! He was trying to tell me something about money and ... that some people were going to ... try to do something."

"Nothing else? No one else?"

"Some Indios. They were arguing with Sarah about making her go to the hospital or something on that order."

"Pancho and some of the others were trying to get Sarah to let them bring you here. She refused. I had to go out there and take you out of the house and bring you here. Pancho came to me and said you were in bad shape and she wouldn't let you get to treatment."

"Pancho is a friend, I think. I don't think my dear wife is. All she cares about is making money and impressing all her snotty friends. I begin to think she doesn't give a shit if I live or die."

"To tell the truth, that was my impression."

"She'll give you nothing but trouble."

"Oh, she's very impressed and it was all somebody else's fault she acted like she did, but, you see, everyone was after her money! She just didn't have *any* idea of who she could trust! She just *knows* she can trust *me*!"

"What? You're a multimillionaire recluse or something, and she found out about it?"

"The Greenwoods, Auermonds, and Grossman were here. Doc wouldn't let them see you. All they could talk about was money – which we peons without a pot or window wouldn't understand. Doc said I understood a little about money. I'd donated six million or so to the hospitals."

"Did you?" he asked.

"Uh-huh. What he didn't tell them was that I only

arranged for the funds because of cases."

"She didn't piss in her pants when he said 'six million' did she?"

"She might have. She looked like she had."

He laughed. "Spread it on thick! I think, just maybe, she's the one who hit me. She's worried that we can't pay back the money the others put in the project. I want to be rid of her."

"If you die, the bills are all paid – but not if it's murder. She has to arrange for you to die by what can be called natural causes."

He looked thoughtful, then suddenly was asleep. Clint left, went to the morgue, and told Doc about the conversation, then headed home.

"Clint? Sergio here. What happened with that Morris thing?" It was two days later. Morris was scheduled to get out of the hospital today. He was going to stay in an apartment he'd rented, with Clint's help. He didn't care to go back to Popa. He could say the doctor ordered that he come to the hospital for checkups every day for five, then every other for six, then once a month, if all was well.

"Nothing new. He saw the other partners for about fifteen minutes, yesterday afternoon. Doc said they could stay ten minutes, because it was business. If they came because they gave a damn about the patient, they could have stayed a half hour. He had arranged that with Morris."

"Those people... have no respect for anyone. They are *not* liked by the staff at Swan's Cay. They're demanding. Nothing is ever what they wanted. You would think, at the price they were paying, they could get a little service, now and then.

"I said tell them they're getting every service promised in the registration. If they wanted more, they could arrange for it at their own expense. They seem to have enough money to pay for extra services."

"They don't have, as they said about me, a pot or window. It's costing them more than they can afford to be here, at all. It's just a front. It's all on charge cards."

"Some Germans asked Evelyn how people could accumulate so much money and never learn how to act in public. Where they could overhear. They also managed to let them know they were German when they were at the next table having dinner with Marty Gold, the lawyer.

That would send them a mixed message!"

"What does Marty think of them?"

"He'd like to slow-fry the lot."

They talked a bit, then Sergio asked that Clint make a report about going out there to take Robert to the hospital. They had asked if he really was working with the police. A report would make it official. "Just something like; went to Isla Popa and transported a crime victim, Robert Morris, to the hospital in Bocas del Toro, Isla Colon. Wife and son objected strongly. Needs investigation. That will scare the piss out of her!"

Clint agreed, sat down to write a short report, then went to the station and filed it. He then went around town, talking to friends. He met Marty Gold at the Golden Grill, who said those people had tried to hire him to check on Clint and the police.

"Take the money. I filed a report about it."

"Deal!" he said, grinning. "How about two hundred bucks per hour, one hour minimum.

"Oh, give them a break. Seeing they're new here, only ninety bucks an hour."

They laughed. He went on. After awhile, he decided to go fishing for an hour or so to relax. When he got back, he got a call from Sergio. He said Marty had gotten a copy of the report. He had put a stamp on it before making the copy and had put Clint down as "Special consultant and deputy, Clint Faraday, Bocas del Toro" on the report identification line. They laughed about Marty letting them wheedle him down to seventy five dollars. It was the kind of thing lawyers did for twenty to twenty five dollars, regularly.

Clint and Judi went to El Ultimo Refugio for dinner and to hear Dave and friends perform some music. Judi met a friend she dated on a semi-regular basis. Clint met a woman from David, a friend of Dave's, who spent the rest of the night with him.

He went to visit Robert the next morning, to find him a lot better and in good spirits. He was going to tell Sarah and William they could go back to the states, but he was staying in Panamá until something could be worked out about the project. The Greenwoods and Auermonds were yelling about suing him for the loss. Grossman was trying to find a way to get his money back. He, at least, knew there was no way to sue anyone because of a bad investment.

"I still think it was Sarah who hit me, though it could have been William."

"I wouldn't be surprised at either or both," Clint agreed. "Trouble is, we can't get any proof, even as to who gave you poison. They can claim there was antifreeze there and you must have gotten something that was contaminated, by accident. Any path of investigation without more is a dead end. There's simply not enough proof to present for a denunciado."

He nodded. The way that whole bunch was fixated solely on money, it might have been a cooperative effort to get the insurance money. William had even said that it was a good thing Clint brought him to the doctor. He checked. There wouldn't be any insurance if he'd died from a murder attempt.

"He had miscalculated that, too, hunh?" Clint asked.

"I would say! I can't believe I let her turn my son into that ... thing. I hope I never see either of them again. That goes for the rest of them. I have enough income from royalties on ads I produced to keep me going pretty well, here. There's the house and dock. It's comfortable."

Clint agreed. He went back home, then took his boat past Chiriqui Grande to visit friends on the comarca. He spent the night, then headed back to Bocas Town. As soon as he was in range, his phone buzzed. Judi. It seemed there had been an accident. Sarah and William had somehow turned off the main road to David and had run over the end of the short road there for heavy equipment used in repairs. They didn't read Spanish, so didn't know it was marked as a private road, that access was prohibited. When the equipment wasn't there, the paved lot dropped directly into a little valley, seventy meters below.

"Talk about a dead end!" she finished.

"I think it's not that simple. Now I have to investigate what really happened.

"Are the Grossman crowd still there?"

"The Greenwoods. The rest went to Panamá City yesterday."

Clint chatted a few minutes, then turned in at Chiriqui Grande and caught the David bus. He knew the road into the lot up in the mountains at Palo Seco. There was no way anyone wouldn't know that was a service road.

"I'd like to know what happened with the accident in Palo Seco. The gringos?" Clint asked at the checkpoint at La Mina/Hornitos.

"I went up there. Ask me, it was no accident. That kid – or somebody else – drove off the lot, deliberately."

"The kid was driving?"

"Strapped in behind the wheel. She wasn't strapped in, but that would hardly matter. Air bags aren't much good when you hit upside down after a drop of seventy meters."

"I guess not! Thanks."

"Want to know something else? I can tell you as a fellow

cop."

"What?"

"We're looking into a few little things – like the fact the transmission was in neutral, for one small example."

"Anything to identify who did it?"

"We have a handprint, but couldn't prove it had anything to do with that, even though there's no other reason it would be over other prints on the transmission shift lever."

"Whose?"

"We don't know. We have one like it from an accident three years ago."

"Pro. Somebody hired him."

"I'd say."

Clint went to the site, then back into David. It looked like the insurance would pay double if they died in an accident. The fact he could bring the "accident" part into serious question meant it wouldn't pay, at all. He might just do that!

He went to Dave's apartment in David for the night. He knew the places to look for the kind of person who would make an "accident" happen like that. There was a little bar near the David fairgrounds that he'd been in before, then there were the places like two near Pedrigal. He got a couple of hints, but it wasn't quite the type of thing they did. They usually would make it seem a mugging that got out of hand or a house fire that trapped someone inside. If the hit man was hired in Bocas, it wouldn't be known here, except through those in the same business. He went back to David and sacked out, then caught the bus back to Chiriqui Grande at 7:00 in the morning, picked up his boat, and was back home by two thirty. He went to talk with Sergio, nothing, and to Morris. Morris said he didn't know anything, except that they had taken a dive off a cliff in the rented car that William was supposed to be driving.

"He might have been, but he's just seventeen and recently got his learner's permit. He drove too fast and a bit carelessly the two times I allowed him to drive with me in the car. It seems suspicious, but I don't really much care. I think I was finally over her since I woke up in the hospital here. I haven't gotten along with William since he was thirteen and she began to treat him like the undisputed king of the household. Most of the trouble I had with her was over him.

"I guess it's a good part my fault. I was working ten to fourteen hours a day and was dead tired at night. I let her take total control over him. She let him rule her.

"She spent so much on him, a part of which was bailing him out of trouble all the time, that I have the hidden account I can live on. If I sell the place, I can pay everybody back. I'm not going to be in a hurry to sell, though. I do like the area and do like the people, now that I treat them like people and they treat me like a person. I can continue the ad business on the net. It won't be as much, but it'll pay the bills, with a little for a good restaurant once in a while.

"I can't believe I was becoming what I was becoming. That bunch came in here yesterday and never asked how I felt, even. All they wanted to do was get their money back or they'd sue and ruin me.

"I told them to go for it. The contract was for investment. The investment failed. I could tell them to stick it, or they could wait until I sold the place to get a part of it back. I think Fatty's the only one who understands it."

"You know they didn't go over that cliff, they were sent, don't you?" Clint asked.

"Interesting way of putting it. I was right here. I didn't

do it."

"Grossman and the Auermonds are gone. The Green-woods are still here."

"I don't think Fatty would do anything like that. If it's any of them, it's the Auermonds. They don't have a line to cross whenever it comes to getting more money. If the Greenwoods are here, it was the Auermonds."

"It was a hired job. It could be any of you."

"I guess I have motive, but I swear, I didn't do it. I was right here and don't have a clue, when it comes to hired killers."

"You all have motive. They die in an accident, Sarah anyhow, and the double indemnity pays off all the invest-ment bills."

"In that case, I'll keep the place and tell that bunch in Oklahoma to kiss my royal rusty ass!"

"It won't pay. It was no accident. They don't pay out anything for murder or such."

"Then I'm no better off than I was."

They chatted awhile, then Clint went home to ask Judi if there was anymore news.

"The Greenwoods are going back to the states tomorrow. Nobody knows where Grossman is. The Auermonds are in Panamá City. That's about it. No other gossip that's any-thing we haven't already covered."

"I guess I'll have to dig to find which of them did it. I'm not the type to let it pass. Not this. With those mafia types, it's better for the country that they go and kill each other off somewhere else. These people are just too disgustingly sordid for me to ever let it go. The Auermonds and Greenwoods. Grossman – I'm on the fence about. He isn't quite as low as the others."

"That's not saying a lot."

He nodded. She grinned and shook her head. They changed the subject and discussed the way the seasons seemed to be changing in just a few years. Then Clint went home.

How to trace this to one specific person was becoming a challenge. It was coming down to finding the hit man and breaking him down. Clint wanted to know who was behind it for reasons other than just catching someone who killed someone else – even if it *could* be shown they deserved worse.

Next step was finding that hit man. It was a dead end there, if he couldn't be found and identified. They would never know for certain which one was behind it. Clint wanted to know more because Robert was staying in Panamá than for other reasons. If he was behind it, there was no way Clint wouldn't insist on prosecution. If it was one or more of the others he wanted them permanently barred from coming back to Panamá, for any reason or at any time.

Funny how your ideas changed in another place with another culture. Clint looked on this kind of thing as a problem that should be handled by the place they came from, not the place they pulled their shit. It involved gringos, not Panamanians – so why should Panamá have to pay for housing and feeding them? It was a more pragmatic outlook in a more pragmatic (in some ways) culture. The Indios were certainly pragmatic people, to the point they seemed more fatalistic, at times.

Quit stalling. Find the assassin.

Clint had ways to find who would be behind this kind of thing in Bocas more than in David. He would start in Changuinola and work to Chiriqui Grande, or even Mali, though his hired pro would be from Changuinola or Bocas.

Probably a transplant or regular visitor from Colon or

certain sections of Panamá City.

He went to his own car in Almirante and drove to Changuinola to ask around. He had some friends who were on the shady side of the law there, as well as some Indio friends who would hear and remember things, even if they never did mention them.

Two days later, he had three names, one of whom was supposed to be good at the automobile accident methods. This one was from Colon. He came to Changuinola for more than half the year. His name was "Tigre" Taylor. He wasn't liked or trusted by anyone not in his immediate family. He was a violence freak and an arrogant SOB, according to almost everyone who knew him.

Clint finally found him in a little bar that catered to blacks. The reputation wasn't among the best places for genteel folks.

Clint went in and asked who he was. He was big and wore dredlocks. He was sitting with a girl who looked like she would rather be someplace else. There was no one sitting close to them, so Clint took a stool next to the girl with him, against the wall at the end of the bar. He ordered a Balboa, they only had Atlas, so he took one and sat back to look around the place in the small mirror behind the bar. It was a place he might come in the front door, but not a place he would stay, usually.

"Give us a drink here!" Tigre called to the barmaid. "The fucking gringo's gonna pay for them."

"Like shit!" Clint returned. "In fact, you're going to pay for this one, hotshot."

"If I say you'll pay, you'll pay!"

"Same here. I guess we'll have to see how this one turns out, huh? I guarantee you'll regret getting in my face!"

"You know who I am, gringo?"

"You're some self-important asshole I came across in a cheap bar. You're probably one of those people from Colon who think they're bad-asses. You're usually pussy-asses. Somebody stands up to you and you back down like a rabbit facing a beagle."

He stood and came toward Clint, who smirked at him. The barmaid said, "Tigre! No aqui!"

"I'll have to put it off, gringo. You better watch where you go from now on!" Tigre said.

Clint laughed. "Like a rabbit facing a beagle!"

Tigre grabbed at him – and came to five minutes later, laying on the floor, staring at the ceiling. When he lunged at Clint, Clint decked him with a hard shot to the jaw. He wanted this to happen, because there was a very definite pecking order among this type. He was now the "A" male. The barmaid started to come around at the same time Tigre went for Clint. Clint waved at her as soon as Tigre hit the floor and said it was all over. Just a little misunderstanding about who was the real bad-ass and who was a big wimp who intimidated people into thinking he was a man.

She let a grin escape and bought him a beer. She said Tigre was a pain in the ass. She was damned glad some-body finally stood up to show everyone else what he was.

"He's probably a bad-ass among people who're just like him. All mouth and bluff and no spine or ass. Anything he does, he sneaks around with. He's a carbon copy of half the bad-asses from Colon. He made the mistake of challenging someone else without six of his buddies along – though I wouldn't have cared if they were. They're all alike."

"He's a professional killer!" the girl cried. "You better watch your back!"

"My back is the only place he'll try to attack from," Clint agreed. "I think, after living more than fifty five years, I can watch my back for this kind of crud."

Tigre was coming around, Clint smirked at him and said he could use some lessons in matching his actions with his mouth. That was 'way out of balance at the moment.

"You'll wish you'd never been born, before long!" Tigre snarled.

"Want another go? I'll lay a hurting on you that'll show, next round. Third round, you take the long dive. Capich?"

This exchange with Tigre had been in English. The other patrons didn't know the words, but knew what was being said. Tigre didn't know how to react to anyone who was standing up to him, depending on his size and reputation to keep anyone from actually moving against him. He was fidgeting and didn't know how to regain his reputation as a bad-ass.

"Don't let your stupid mouth get you in any deeper than you are. Don't pull this bad-ass shit on anyone else, particularly gringos. A lot of us grew up in cities that make Colon look like Pleasantville. If you live as long as I have, you can handle amateur wannabes.

"I suppose most gringos here are retirees from better places. They came to get away from places like that and people like you. The problem you'll have is that, just once in awhile, you'll get in the face of someone like me, who grew up on the streets. Take a lesson when it's offered You'll live longer and have a lot less problems in life.

"Now that we've broken the ice, you the one who knocked over that fucking idiot spoiled brat and his lovely mother?"

"No. That was from Bocas. You don't ... you knew who I am and what I do when you started this?"

"I didn't start it. I finished it. I knew you'd play the bad-ass and would do exactly what you did.

"Who in Bocas?"

"I don't know. One of those brothers who hang around the VIP, I think."

"That figures!"

Clint bought him a beer, said it was as much as a setup to find out if he was the one who should get a reward for purging the Earth of those two. He accepted the beer and asked if he could make it look like they had it set up. It was an act. They did it before.

"See, if they think I can take a KO and get up and laugh about it, they won't start getting in my face all the time."

Clint shrugged. Tigre slapped him on the back and laughed. Loud. Clint grinned and shook his head. He looked at the patrons, who didn't know how to take this turn of events. "El es loco, pero is okay. Yo tambien!" Clint announced. "Es mejor el conoce donde es la fila. No cruce!" (he's crazy, but that's okay. I am too. It's better he knows where the line is and that he doesn't cross it.)

Clint finished his beer and waved goodbye to everyone and left. He went back to Almirante, got his boat, and went to Bocas Town. He had plenty of time to clean up and get a good meal before he would go to the VIP. It didn't get started until about 9:30.

There were about six people at the VIP when Clint walked in and ordered a Balboa. They were out, so he took a Panama, which was also a good beer.

Clint knew several people, there. They were always around somewhere in Bocas Town. Most of them were fairly decent people, but a few of them were the worst kinds of thugs. Almost all of them were blacks. Several were from Colon. Colon is the only dangerous place in Panamá, except for one section of Panamá City. The present president was trying to clean up Panamá City, but the last five or six presidents have given up on Colon. They suggest on their international website that tourists (or anyone else) stay away from Colon. The thugs here depended on the reputation of Colon to intimidate people. Clint knew that they were the type who had to have several, enough to outnumber the ones they were molesting, or they would be the nicest people you could meet. The type disgusted him, but that was a common type on all the Caribbean islands and adjoining mainlands.

He knew the type he was looking for. He also knew he wouldn't get any direct information *because* they knew him. They also knew he couldn't be intimidated. That would work in his favor.

He chatted with a couple of the girls, then with Rocko and Streeter. (Their parents picked names from rap music), two from Colon who were always together. Clint figured, as popular as they'd made themselves, they'd be dead if they weren't together. They said they didn't have anything to do with knocking over the gringos. That wasn't their style and they weren't about to tell Clint Faraday whose style it was.

Clint grinned at Streeter, who had just made the statement. "That's because you don't have a clue. You aren't ones any of them would trust while they were looking at you."

They'd been digging at each other for some time. This was looked on as a joke between friends. Clint had said that "Many a truth is said in jest." – but that went a mile over their heads.

Marchesca came in, a local drag queen whose real name was Nicolo. Clint could probably get more information from him than any of the others, but would have to do it very discreetly.

"Hi, Clint! Buy me a rum and Coke?"

Clint waved to Lydia and pointed to him. She brought the drink. Clint asked what was new.

"Well, other that some real bad-ass in Changuinola dumped Tigre, not much. Of all the people in Changuinola who deserve dumping, and they number in the hundreds, he was top of the list. He's a creep! Can't keep his hands off you, then pretends he won't even stay in the same room with a gay. Stupid fucking piece of shit is probably gay, himself. Why else would he always be pawing at transvestites like me?

"What a thrill! Big Bad Brucie-woosie, in person!"

"Yeah. He broke bad with me. All I did was go in for a beer. It was hot as hell over there this morning."

"He tells everybody you two are friends and always try to get the best of each other. Sometimes he decks you, sometimes you deck him. You're both man enough to take a little dumping from a friend in a good spirit."

"We're friends about like chickens and boa constrictors. He thought he had some old geezer he could intimidate and make himself look like a real bad-ass instead of a cheap copy wannabe. He tried to intimate he was the one who clocked the gringo punk and his mom."

"Shit! That was probably Anderson or Rico. Tigre – and that's a bigger joke than the rest of him – doesn't do anything, himself. He finds people who will, for a fee. I'm more actual macho than he'll ever be."

"I sort of figured Rico. I'm not familiar with Anderson."

"He's that really big one, in more than one sense, from Panamá City. The one with the gold chains all over the place. He's man enough to say he likes sex and doesn't care who it's with, so long as they know what they're doing. He considers me an expert!"

"I've heard you really are."

"Well, Ben has you so tied up with the gay stuff that I can't get a chance, but I'll be glad to demonstrate anytime you're feeling lonely and unloved!"

They chatted awhile. Clint moved away when a tourist came in and looked over the place. Marchesca moved right in and said he'd show him the best side of town.

"You're a guy in a dress! I'm not gay!" the man cried.

"I wouldn't be interested, if you were. Where are you from?"

Clint grinned to himself and went outside, where several people were sitting on the curb (such as it was) across the street, smoking. Smoking isn't allowed anywhere in Panamá where anyone else will be in the smoke. That's all restaurants, bars, stores, parks, etc. Clint doubted very much that the police would check a place like the VIP for smokers. He chatted with several about general things. They didn't say anything he wanted to hear about anybody, but he had a place to start looking. Anderson, who he didn't know and Rico, who he'd met and been unimpressed.

He went next door to where they were sitting and into El Ultimo Refugio for a good late meal and to talk with various people. Not much was happening, so he went to the Toro Loco, which was about the same, then to the Rip Tide, to find the boat was gone. Neal and Cathy had broken up and she owned the landing, but Neal the boat. She was running the restaurant on the land, now.

He finally went home about twelve thirty. Anything else could wait until morning.

Clint laid in the hammock on his deck with his coffee and hojaldres he'd fixed. He had some spaghetti sauce from a couple of days before in the fridge, so used it as a sort of dip for the hojaldres. It was damned good!

He had to look up Anderson and Rico. He figured he would know which one by what they were doing now.

Judi came onto her deck and waved and shook a finger at Clint. That was as much as a ritual, anymore. He didn't wear anything until he decided what he would do for the day. He waved and called that he would probably be around for the next day or two, at least. His case was at a standstill. She waved back and said, "Regular!"

He finished the semi-breakfast and went into town to talk with the regular people at the Golden Grill and other regular stops. Don Chicho's and Chitres. Nothing much new. There was some talk about the dead gringos, but few of the people ever met them. They were the type who didn't mix with the natives. The few who met the punk said he always seemed to have a chip on his shoulder about one thing or another.

Without asking, he found that Anderson was living just off 6th street with Arnie and Jorge Salinas, also from Colon and they wished he'd go back and take them with him. Judi had taught him how to drop a little piece of information and move on. A lot of times, someone else with a gripe or knowledge or something would say something. You act like, that's interesting, did you plan to go to the Orchid Fair in Boquete?

They would just have to expand on it to impress you with what they knew.

Clint said he'd heard there were a couple of real thugs from Colon on the island. Supposed to be hired killer type. He wished there was some way to get them out before they did something that Sergio could use to bar them from Isla Colon. He then said the fishing was pretty good down by Tierra Oscura and the islands, there, clear out to the Zapatillas. Jim had connected that in his mind with the gringos they had mentioned earlier. Anderson occurred to him immediately as a likely type to have killed them.

So. Clint knew where he would find Anderson. Rico would be on Bastimentos in the mornings and come to Bocas Town about three nights a week, so he would be easy to find.

Clint went home to catch everything there up to date, then went back to town and to The Reef Restaurant. Anderson would hang around the dock, outside. A lot of that type would, because the tourists liked the restaurant. They could start conversations and learn if they had anything worth stealing or could hire themselves out as gigolos. Clint always told people coming in that he met to stop showing around their expensive cell phones and cameras or those were two items that would disappear. Laptops, even more.

Anderson wasn't there, but Rico was on the island taxi docks, talking with Guillermo, who wasn't interested in what he was offering. Clint happened to walk by and greet Guillermo. Rico said "Hola!" and walked back off the dock to stand by the gate. He obviously wanted to talk to Clint, so a few words later, he went back to the gate.

"Clint, I just want you to know I didn't have anything to do with the gringos going over the cliff. Marchesca told me you seemed interested in it."

"I'm just that. Interested. Nothing I'm going to waste a lot of time on. I don't want to tag whoever did it, but I'd like to know which one of those greedy clowns arranged it."

"It was some woman. She was asking about who to get to do a job that wasn't entirely legal and would end up ending someone up."

"The gringa? Which one – and don't answer if you've made any promises or whatever. I'm just curious."

"That one who went over. The Sarah bitch. That's why I don't understand it."

Clint nodded. "She probably wanted her dear husband knocked off. Someone else wanted her knocked off. Maybe she found the hit man who hit her, which would be a real giggle."

"It would be that!" He saw a woman who looked lost. A tourist. He grinned at Clint and asked her what she was looking for. She said some place called "The Gourmet." It was almost across the street, but they were building a hotel next door that hid the signs. Rico showed her the place and went inside with her. She managed to grin at Clint, so she knew what she was doing. She was a middle-aged woman who wanted a good time, Rico was a goodlooking native who spoke English, she could act like she had a lot of money and he would romance her to get some. Everyone would get part of what they wanted. Go for it!

So. Sarah found a hit man. She was plotting with at least one of the others to knock over her husband. Her husband was staying out of reach. She became the next best bet to get that insurance payout. It would have worked, but for a handprint on a gearshift knob.

Clint knew Anderson made the hit. He didn't know which of the survivors was behind it. Even Robert could have found out about it and could have made a deal with that hit man to hit the one trying to have him hit. That would be un-poetic justice! She found her own hit man!

It would be easy enough to prove Anderson did the job, to Clint, though the proof wouldn't be usable in court: He would have money. The type didn't do anything but party, if they had money – until it was gone, then they'd be looking for another "job" to have another big splash on. Anderson hadn't been in Bocas Town for three nights. He'd gone to Changuinola, where he could find a lot more parties that would appeal to him than he could in Bocas Town.

Clint went to Changuinola and to the places where he would be known. He had gone to David. He had a lot of money and couldn't find any excitement in Changuinola.

Clint drove to David and went to the spots. Anderson had been to The Esmeralda one night, hadn't found a girl he particularly liked, and had left. He was in two places in Pedrigal, then said this was nothing but shit and had gone to Las Tablas.

Clint figured there wasn't anything in Las Tablas that would attract him more than David, which meant Colon or Panamá City.

Not Colon. If he showed up there with money, his own type would soon relieve him of it. Clint headed for Panamá City. He would stay away from the worst parts of town there for the same reasons he wouldn't go to Colon. He'd probably go to the more expensive tourist places at night, but would stay in the suburbs during the day.

Clint wondered if it was worth it, then decided it was something to do, so went to two places before deciding Anderson would go the casino route in Panamá City. He didn't in David, because he would be watched, there. David had some bad experiences with people from Colon several years back and made it plain they weren't welcome.

He had been in the Fiesta the night before, had won a couple hundred dollars and had connected with one of the "ladies" who frequented the place. It was very likely he'd be back that night. He came in about ten the first time, so that might be a pattern. Clint would be there at ten.

There he was! He fit the description, perfectly. He was wearing some new expensive clothes and showing a little money. Clint knew damned well he'd know not to show much. He wondered how much he'd left out for the woman of last night to take.

Clint waited until he was sitting at the end of the upstairs bar with an empty stool on either side to go sit next to him and say, "Anderson. Bocas."

"And you?"

"Faraday, almost anywhere in Panamá."

"Oh, shit! Look. I might have done a job, but it wasn't anything like, I mean ... Oh, shit!"

"I'm not after you. Calm down. I just want to know which one or ones should be asked to leave Panamá. Permanently."

"First was some woman on the phone who wanted me to get rid of her husband. He was squandering everything they had. I think it was about some other woman or two of them or something. I asked her who and she told me it was some guy who someone tried to kill on Isla Popa, so it could be made to look like part of that. They'd get the insurance that would bail them out of trouble and be rid of him at the same time.

"I heard about that, and that the cops were watching every move he made and would catch me, so no thanks.

"The other, I don't know. It was by notes, with half down and half when it was done. I figured, 'What the hell? Why not?' I figured it right then that the same one to get wasted was the one who wanted me to go after her husband. It was just something that, Christ! I just turned the job on her. I don't know who was behind it. The note said this one was going to David and would be the only one going in a rented car, then."

Clint nodded. "Where were the notes delivered? By whom?"

"While I was at The Reef, on the dock. A kid came and said the man said to give me the note and he'd get a quarter. He spoke English and the note was in English, so there wasn't much chance an Indio kid about ten years old could read it.

"I picked up the cash down, five hundred, at The Reef, next day, after I sent the kid back with another quarter to tell the man maybe I would be interested.

"Next was another kid with a note that said what he wanted and that I could collect the down at The Reef on the dock the next day at three, when there wasn't anybody around. It would be in a dirty carryout box in the garbage can.

"I watched the place from the road. I didn't see when it was put there, but it was there, with instructions, so I did the job. He probably came in a boat to leave it, so I couldn't see from the road. That was all."

"It was someone who knew the car and where it would go?"

"Yeah. It was a rented Honda and would be on the way to David with two people, one male, one female, and would be the only one going then. I could watch for it at the restaurant where the buses stop because the people would want to get something to eat before going on to David. I could manage something from that point they didn't want to know about. If the job was done, the money would be delivered in a sack with my name on it in David. I was to be in the bus terminal there at six in the morning, if I wasn't contacted with the payment before then.

"I thought I'd probably missed them because it was almost an hour late when they showed up. Anyhow, it was right there in the car! They managed to have the payment hidden there, where nobody would look for it, so I'd never see them at the terminal or something. They could figure I'd look through the car to see if there was anything that would, er, point to me, you see.

"I got in when they stopped for the restroom and sodas and hid in the crap in the back seat. They didn't even look back there, just got in and went on. That kid's a terrible driver!

"Anyhow, I waited until past Mali and stuck a pistol in the kid's ear and told him to slow down and drive right or I'd blow his fucking head off. We got up by the construction crap lot and I made him pull in, then rapped him lightly over the ear and smacked her with her damned mouth running all the time pretty good!

"She kept yelling that I had the wrong people. There was some mistake, that she didn't something or other. She was so mad she didn't make much sense and my English stinks and she didn't know Spanish, so I told her to shut the fuck up or I'd blow her head off before the kid's. I told her I just wanted a ride up into the mountains and wouldn't have let them know I was there, even, if the kid knew how to drive. That calmed her down and she said some friends or something had a bad experience when someone tried to hijack them.

"Anyhow, she shut up, more or less, but not for long. She started in again about something or other that her husband caused to happen. She was trying to get me to do something, but it wasn't making any sense again. She was so pissed at the old man she was ranting. I got about every third word. All about costing her everything and he didn't even care. I tuned her out, but was glad to smack her up there.

"I did the job and went back to Bocas. No sense in going to David when I already had what I would go for. I guess they figured that, too. That's all I know."

"Fair enough. Don't take any chances anymore. Doing jobs for anyone except the mob characters will get your ass in a bind you can't get out of. If it was that, I wouldn't bother to even check it out. Seeing it was what it was, I don't give a damn.

"I'll tell you something else, if you'll agree not to mess with those kinds of people, even if they *are* worse than the mob types."

"I figured that when you said your name. I figured my ass was about to get scorched for twenty years. Deal."

"Wear gloves when you shift the gears. You left the second handprint on that knob. If they suspect you of anything else, they'll compare and tag you, just like you figured I would. Also, you keep the promise or they'll get a hint to check your prints for anything anyone did that such a print might solve."

He grinned and said that would make it sure, for sure!

Clint went back to his car. He started giggling before he got there and was almost howling when he did. Sarah had contacted this bird to get her husband knocked off so she could get the insurance. It wasn't possible to have him hit, so she decided to get the Auermonds hit, instead. It would take care of the insurance and she could go back to the states and leave hubby in Panamá.

The Auermonds had left early, or something. He missed them at the bombas – but Sarah had headed to David an hour later, expecting to learn to her horror that the Auermonds had an accident and were dead! She had the rest of the hit's money in a sack, like she promised. She had better sense than to try to stiff a hit man. The Auermonds didn't show, but she did. In a rented Honda. Two people. Neither the man who sent the notes. The kids told him it was a man and they delivered his answer to a man. Anderson was told there would be two people, one male and one female, without telling him their age, in a rented Honda. They would be the only ones coming through then.

Anderson pops out from under whatever in the back seat in the mountains past Mali. There wasn't anything else before the dam. Sarah is livid to the point of incoherence, but thinks she can talk him out of doing anything. She can say the proof is the money in the sack – only he only speaks a little English and she can't say ten words in Spanish.

Then he sounds like some joker running from the law or something who just wants a ride into the mountains. He only let them know he was back there because William is a bad driver. He would get out where he could hide from the police in the mountains.

He tells them to pull into the access road so he can get out, then handles the job. He has the payment he was promised. She'd arranged for it to be right there in the car, where she knew he'd find it! He went back to Bocas, another job done well. Clint wondered if it dawned on her in the last seconds of her life that she'd paid for her own murder.

Now all he had to know was who the man was who had the kids deliver the money. It should be Grossman – but he had disappeared.

Because he didn't want to be around to be identified, if anything went wrong? It could still be Robert. He could have set it up to go down exactly the way it *did* go down. It could be Greenwood, who was there in Bocas town.

That meant finding Grossman. That would resolve it as much as he figured it needed resolution.

"So that's how I figure it happened," Clint finished telling Sergio, Dave and Judi. "Now I have to find Grossman to know if I figured right."

"*And* the Greenwoods *and* the Auermonds," Sergio pointed out.

"I don't give a shit about them. They're going, anyhow, and won't be back here. I'll get word to them through a friend that they're wanted for questioning about a murder if they ever step foot in Panamá again."

"Grossman is going, too," Judi pointed out.

"Probably, but he'd be the type to come back. If he gets away with anything here, he won't worry about being arrested and questioned next trip. He's a lot more savvy about how that works. He knows damned well that there would simply be an order on his name and passport that he was not to be allowed in the country."

"I can have that order inserted," Sergio said. "I can make a report that they are involved with schemes to defraud, which hurts investment and tourism, and that even other gringos don't want them here."

"And Clint wouldn't ever know for sure who had those obnoxious people killed," Judi said. "I think I'd like to know if I figured it right. The important thing is if Robert Morris was the one. That would mean he has to go – right, Clint?"

"That, and I think Manny would like to put something for the Indios on Popa. It's a good location for them to bring bananas, coconuts, coffee, cacao, chickens – what have you – for shipping on to Almirante or Bocas Town. It would save them hours of carrying the stuff, themselves.

They would bring enough there from all those islands and from Tierra Oscura to make it a pretty profitable deal for everyone. Manny has that materials barge that's as much as rusting away where it sits, so he can clean it up and use it in that shallow water."

"I think that might be a good idea," Sergio said. "I'll keep the order to find Grossman out. Maybe he'll show up, now that the insurance part won't happen.

"I have to get back to the station. I'll talk with you later." He waved and went out.

"Do you think Manny would really be interested in that kind of small business?" Judy asked, when Sergio was gone. "I know he might want to set it up so the Indios can run it, but it seems so tiny, compared with the millions he made in the mob business."

"I've talked with him about using that barge. He loves the idea. It'll make most of those mob kingpins know for certain he's not Bocinni. They'll think exactly like you suggested, and the Indios can get a bit of help with it. It's true they spend six or eight hours a day, twice a week, carrying that stuff all the way from there to Almirante. The bulk Manny would carry means a small margin/big volume operation, so it should work out pretty well.

"Now to find Grossman. I wish I had a clue!"

"I might know someone who knows someone who could find out where he is. Flora's meeting with us in about an hour for the street cleanup committee. I'll see what I can do."

Clint didn't doubt for a second she would find something. She always did.

"He's driving a rented car. Flora's husband services them

for Budget, in Changuinola. He left Changuinola and turned the car in at the airport in David. Carlos, the porter for Venture Air, told Edwardo he took a flight to San Blas.

"You would have found all that out, anyhow, but I hope it saves time or something," Judi reported.

"It saves me three days of going to David and finding which agency he used, then which flight he took. You did it in an hour and a half. If it wouldn't screw up both our lives I'd ask you to marry – well, live with me."

She laughed. "We're a hundred fifty meters away from each other, we're in each other's house all the time, now. That's enough."

"I guess I'll go as directly as I can to San Blas. I've never been there. I hear it's a great place. Want to come along?"

"I'm going next month with a friend, so I'll beg off."

Clint nodded and went the hundred fifty meters back to his place, packed a few odd things and went to the airport. He had to go to Changuinola for a flight where there was only one direct on Fridays.

He flew to David, then took the flight that left there three times per week. It left David just an hour after Clint arrived. He'd used the net to book a seat.

The flight was pleasant, except for one middle-aged woman from France, who could find fault with anything you could mention. She was in the seat behind him. He could hear her constant complaining, all the way. When they got off the plane, he couldn't resist asking her why she stayed here in this hell when France was so perfect. No one forced her to come here, did they?

She called the guard over to complain that he was being deliberately rude to her. The guard said there was no law against being rude to people who were rude to you. She didn't know how to take that, but she shut up for ten minutes – until the baggage man was throwing around her expensive suitcases like they were cheap cardboard boxes like the people here were used to, then was furious because the Cunas (native Indios) refused to help her with her luggage. Clint said she was so picky with everything they felt she would find an excuse to not pay them and would accuse them of all sorts of things. If she was going to be a pain in the ass to everyone around her, she could expect a lot of that.

She was looking for a guard to complain about him when he said, "Have a nice day!" and walked away. One of the Indios who spoke English very well walked out with him. He said they got that type about once a month. The word was out about her from the attendant on the flight, so she would find all the taxis were occupied, except for Luis, who kept two. One was a rust-bucket that smelled of old garbage and stale beer. "If she enjoys complaining about every damned thing we will give her a real cause to complain."

Clint high-fived him and asked where the best hotel at reasonable cost was. He was told about a place the natives stay that was cheap, clean and comfortable. There would only be room available for her at the Paraiso Verde, the most expensive one there – unless she had sense enough to get reservations before anyone there met her.

Clint asked about Grossman, saying he would be arrogant and treat them like serfs, but wasn't a tenth as obnoxious as that woman. He described Grossman.

"Yes. Sol. He's not so bad. He said he got a few lessons about being a tourist in Bocas. You?"

"Several people. He's involved in a company that just got scammed out of enough to break all the partners."

"No title?"

"No. It's titled, but is in the wrong place for what they wanted."

"Happens a lot, here! I'll get to the docks for the ferry. I'm Kelvin."

"Clint. Mucho gusto – oh, yeah! Where is Sol staying?"

"Mar Vista." He waved and went toward the dock, where the ferry was just coming into sight. Fifteen minutes before docking.

Clint considered staying at the native pension. He liked the people there one hell of a lot more than he liked the tourists, but he'd be better for what he wanted to stay at the Mar Vista.

They had a room with a balcony adjoining Sol's room. He grinned to himself and went up. The place was better than he really had expected. The view of the ocean beautiful. There was a very good beach, with a breeze coming in off the Caribbean and the hotel had a pool.

Clint could never understand why people would come to the Caribbean with its clean water and only swim in a pool full of chlorine. It didn't make sense to him.

To each his own.

Grossman wasn't there, at the time. It was late afternoon and he would probably be in one of the more popular bars. The floor attendant said he went out most nights and stayed until about eleven. He sometimes had a professional lady with him when he returned.

Clint grinned and said this was the kind of place people wanted to get away from the proper work life. She agreed and said she could get him a woman anytime, so remember her. Clint said he would.

Kelvin was out front of the hotel when he went out. He asked where there was a good restaurant – typical, not tourist. He liked native foods.

"Yet you stay here?"

"Because my business is with someone staying here, so I didn't really have a choice. I want to know the kind of place I like for when I come back. I think I'll come back here, at times. It's really a beautiful place."

They chatted a few minutes, then Clint said he's spring for dinner, if there was a good place they'd both like. He was taken to a small place about half a kilometer from the tourist town, where he got a truly delicious meal.

He went back to the hotel and sacked out. He was up, as always, at five in the morning, and was sitting on his balcony with a pot of coffee, supplied by the hotel, when Grossman wandered out onto the balcony.

"Faraday? Following me?"

"Uh-huh. I have to find out a couple of things."

"Like?"

"Did you arrange for Sarah and William to get knocked over, or was it Greenwood or Auermond who arranged it?"

He stared at Clint for a moment. "Sarah and William? Knocked off?

"I haven't been in touch with any of them. It was getting tiresome for them to keep railing about losing their life savings instead of looking for a way to make a go of something else there. I think we can find something, but I'd rather be able to buy them out, cheap. The insurance will pay them off if any of us die.

"Look, I know you think I'm involved with that, but I'm not! If someone arranged it, it was ... I think only Sarah was that stupid. She wouldn't be dead if she was behind it, though."

"Oh, she set it up to have the Auermonds hit. The hit

man didn't speak English very well and she turned up at the place he was supposed to meet the Auermonds, instead, if a little later. All he knew was she was in a rented Honda, two people, so he thought they were the two people and shoved their car over a cliff with them in it. There was a man as a go-between who delivered instructions. I figure it was you or Greenwood, seeing Auermond was supposed to be the one offed. It could be Robert."

"It wasn't Robert. That leaves Francis. It wasn't me."

Clint looked out at the ocean for a minute, thinking. He believed him. "I like this place. I'll probably come here sometimes."

"What'll you do about Francis?"

"Nothing, It'll be pointedly suggested that he never step foot in Panamá again or he'll be detained for questioning about a murder. For ten years or so. The Auermonds are going to get the same warning. I wanted to know if you should be getting the same one."

"This isn't going to get any insurance for them, is it?"

"No. It was an obvious murder. They don't pay term insurance for murder."

"I suppose I'll eat the loss. I probably won't come back here, anyway. Maybe here, but not near that end of the country."

"I'll help Robert set something up that'll pay enough for him to live. He can try to sell most of the corporation and just keep a hectare or so to live. He has the dock and house there."

"Will it ever sell?"

"If Robert sets up something that pays ... I suppose so. You should get at least half of your investment back in a year or so."

"I can live with that. I can convince the others that it's as good as it's likely to get. They'll be happy with half. It's better than eating the whole magilla."

Clint nodded. "I think I'll stay here another couple of days before going back to Bocas."

"It is nice. Expensive, compared to Bocas, but nice."

Clint nodded again.

"So it was another thing where arrogant SOB's who refused to learn enough Spanish to get by got it back," Clint said. "Anderson knows some English, but it's like when you first learn Spanish. The main phrase you use is, 'Habla despacio, por favor.' (Speak slowly, please) If she hadn't kept ranting, he could have understood her."

"That wasn't her nature," Judy said. "She expected everyone here to learn English. After all, she came here to spend her money, so the least they could do was learn English! She'd be the type to yell about all those Spanish-speaking people coming into the states who wouldn't have the simple sense and decency to learn English. After all! English is the language of the country!"

"She was a pain in the ass to everyone. I finally got over her when I figured it had to be her, William, or both who tried to kill me. It damned well had to be her who tried to poison me!" Robert said. "I look back and see what an insufferable asshole idiot I was, too. As soon as I met the Indios as people instead of savages, they accepted me. I even have two who I consider to be friends."

"Pancho and Sanchos. They're as good friends as you're ever likely to have," Manny said. "You're learning that they're also intelligent, far above the average. That's why we have them as the managers of the transport business. They insisted that we don't buy a lot of expensive equipment to handle the produce. That would mean we had to charge too much for it to make a go. They're perfectly content with carrying a couple of tons of plantains across a dock to the barge, themselves. It's part of what they always did. The price was 'delivered,' which meant they usually had to carry the stuff across town or hire a taxi.

"One lousy month and we're showing a profit. Not much, but you don't expect to show a profit in a new business for two years, as a general rule."

They were on Clint's deck for a get-together a month and a half after Clint returned from San Blas. The Aurmonds and Greenwoods were back in the states, with warnings not to ever come back to Panamá. Grossman might come back to San Blas, sometime, but it wasn't likely. It was expensive and the natives would never mention the pension or native restaurants.

It was a nice enough night. The moon was about 3/4 full and there was a cool breeze off the bay. Judi had fixed a good gumbo with crawdads the Indios brought from the mountains and okra she had growing along one side of her fence.

"Well, we can say goodbye to this one. It did work out pretty well, in the long run," Sergio said.

They had to agree to that!

C. D. Moulton's works are available on most major outlets as printed or e-books. CD writes the CD Grimes, PI, mysteries, the Det. Lt. Nick Storie mysteries, the Clint Faraday mysteries, the Flight of the Maita science fiction series, books on orchid culture and many others of many types. Mystery, adventure, intrigue, science fiction, humor, fantasy, paranormal, mild erotica, and factual.